I0624977

Silk & Silence

A Steamy, Slow-Burn Small-Town Romance About Walls, Wreckage, and the Kind of Love That Finds You When You Stop Hiding

Hana York

Pink Pop Publishing

Silk & Silence

(The Thorne Sisters Book 2)

Copyright © 2025 by Hana York

www.HanaYork.com

Contents

Prologue

VIVIAN

The mirror never lied.

But it was damn good at keeping secrets.

I leaned closer, smoothing a hand over the sequins clinging to my hips, nudging a stray strand of hair back into place. Stage lights didn't forgive. They amplified. Every crack, every flaw, every weakness. And I'd learned how to hide them all.

The Velvet Room was my domain—red velvet, old jazz, and just enough glitter to blur the sharp edges. Classy. Controlled. Untouchable.

Just like I had to be.

Because the second you let someone see the cracks, they started looking for the exit.

I knew that better than anyone.

Pretty was protection.

Youth was survival.

Love? Love was a liability.

I capped the lipstick with a click, sealing the final layer into place.

The color was perfect.

The smile, even better.

No one in the audience would see anything but the woman I built from scratch—the woman who didn't need anyone.

And if, sometimes, my chest tightened a little too sharply?

If I caught myself wondering what it might feel like to be wanted for more than a flawless curve or a polished smile?

Well. Some things you just learned to live with.

A knock came at the dressing room door.

Showtime.

I stood, ran my hands down the sequined fabric one last time, and became the woman the world couldn't break.

The real Vivian Thorne?

She stayed locked away.

Safe.

Untouched.

And very, very alone.

Chapter One

DEAN

I hated days like this.

Days when professionalism took a back seat to spectacle.

"Come to the Velvet Room," my client had said as if it was the most reasonable request in the world. Middle of the afternoon on a workday. Meet me at a damn burlesque club.

Christ.

I'd argued. Suggested neutral ground. A restaurant. A coffee shop. Hell, the courthouse steps would've been preferable. But he insisted. Apparently, he felt "more comfortable" there.

Which, considering how his marriage was ending, said a hell of a lot more than he realized.

I shoved open the door, bracing myself for... hell, I didn't even know. Neon lights. Pulsing music.

Something I'd have to mentally scrub off afterward.

Instead, I got elegance: dark wood floors, vintage tables, and velvet curtains. It didn't smell like cheap beer or sweat. It smelled like old whiskey, expensive perfume, and something else, something rich and deliberate.

I frowned. Suspicious.

Places like this didn't exist without a catch.

I spotted my client, Charlie, waving like he hadn't just detonated the last scrap of my dignity. But before I could force myself forward, something caught at the edge of my vision. Movement from the stage.

And then I saw her.

A woman mid-performance—moving like a goddamn force of nature.

Tall. Poised. She was draped in sapphire sequins that caught the light with every sway of her hips.

But it wasn't the outfit. It wasn't even the body.

It was the *command.*

She wasn't playing to the crowd. She owned the room like she didn't need anyone's approval.

I wasn't prepared for her. Not her presence. Not her power. She moved across that stage like she owned the world, and for one breathless second, everything else fell away. The case. The client. The noise in my head.

Gone.

Only her.

And I was absolutely, without a doubt, screwed.

I tore my gaze away and stalked toward my client, jaw tight.

Focus.

Handle the meeting. Get the papers signed and get out.

That was the plan.

But it was hard to remember what the hell I was supposed to be doing when her laughter—a low, smoky sound—cut through the air and wrapped itself around my chest like barbed wire.

I dropped into the chair beside Charlie, forcing myself into something resembling professionalism.

"We had to meet here?" I muttered under my breath, scanning the room.

Charlie—already two drinks in, judging by the flush on his cheeks—grinned and waved toward the stage. "Relax,

Thatcher. I know it's not your usual vibe, but some of us need a little glitter to get through divorce proceedings."

I pulled the paperwork out of my briefcase and set it between us.

"Sign here. Initial there."

He barely glanced at it—still craning his neck toward the stage.

"You should stick around. Loosen up. Might do you good."

Against my better judgment, my gaze drifted back toward the stage—and caught another glimpse of dark hair, bare shoulders, and a smile that could wreck a man without even trying.

No.

Absolutely not.

"I'm billing you for the full hour either way," I said flatly.

He just laughed and clapped me on the back, completely unfazed.

And me?

I was already planning my escape.

Before, I did something *really* foolish.

Like ask for her name.

Charlie signed with a careless flick of his pen and shoved the folder back toward me.

"That's Vivian," he said, nodding toward the stage. "She runs the place."

I followed his gaze.

"She usually comes out to say hi after her set," Charlie added. "You should stick around. I'll introduce you."

I tapped the folder against the table. Pretended like I wasn't intrigued.

Yes, I wanted to meet her.

No, I absolutely should not.

Because something about her pressed against every boundary I'd built.

And I didn't know what scared me more, the idea of losing control or the realization that maybe I wanted to.

VIVIAN

The last notes of the music faded, the red velvet curtains sweeping back into place behind me.

Another afternoon, another show.

The crowd had been good—lively but respectful. A little loud during the feather fan tease, but that was to be expected.

I grabbed my robe from the backstage hook, shrugging it on as I moved toward the wings.

Viv," Claire called, slipping through the back hall to meet me. "Charlie's hoping you'll stop by and say hi. He's got some Suit with him."

I tugged the robe tighter around my waist and moved toward my dressing room.

A Suit.

I already knew who she meant.

I'd spotted him halfway through my set—new, out of place, impossible to miss.

Dark hair. A jawline you could cut glass on. Shoulders that deserved better than a suit and a starched button-down.

The kind of man who probably said things like *irrevocable trust* for a living.

Most of our patrons relaxed once the lights dimmed—jackets unbuttoned, posture uncoiled, the day's sharp edges dulling into something easier to carry.

Not him.

He sat straight-backed and still.

Not leering.

Not dazzled.

Just... watching.

And if I'd been smart, I would've left it at that.

Noted. Filed away. Forgotten.

But something in the way he watched—calm, unshaken, like he wasn't impressed or intimidated—made him more dangerous than the ones who couldn't stop staring.

The obvious ones? Easy to predict. Easy to ignore.

Men like him?

Men like him were dangerous.

I changed out of my costume. Nothing dramatic—just traded the tease for tailored power.

Slacks that hugged just right. A plunging blouse I wore like a dare.

Charlie spotted me first, waving from one of the corner tables. I smiled for him—polished, easy—and crossed the room like I wasn't bracing for impact.

And then I saw him up close.

God help me.

Crisp lines. Focused stillness. The kind of presence that didn't demand attention—it simply expected it.

When I approached, he stood—*stood*—like we were at some country club luncheon, and he was about to pull out my chair. Polite. Sharp. Unshakable.

Very, very dangerous.

"Vivian," Charlie said, all charm and good intentions. "I wanted to introduce you to a friend of mine. Dean Thatcher."

Dean.

I smiled, cool and easy, and extended my hand.

"Vivian Thorne."

His hand closed around mine. His handshake was firm. Measured. Like everything else about him. No squeeze. No flex. No unnecessary performance.

And for just a moment—just a blink—I saw something in his eyes.

Not lust.

Not conquest.

Recognition.

Like he saw past the performance and the stage lights straight to the woman still standing there.

He released my hand slowly, offering a small, polite smile.

"Nice to meet you." The words were even, careful—like he was trying not to reveal too much.

And God help me again because all I could think was: This man could ruin me without ever laying a hand on me.

Charlie said something—probably trying to fill the air between us—but I barely caught it.

Something about business. About Dean being a lawyer. About how he was just visiting.

Visiting.

Good.

Maybe he'd leave before I did something unwise.

Like, wonder how that voice would sound without all the restraint—just him, unguarded. Then I tucked a curl behind my ear and smiled like he hadn't just turned the ground beneath my stilettos to quicksand.

"Welcome to the Velvet Room," I said, pitching my voice low and smooth. "Hope the show wasn't too scandalous for you."

"Hardly," he said. "More... unexpected."

Something in the way he said it, quiet and sincere, slipped past my defenses before I could stop it, knocking something loose inside me.

I tilted my head, studying him like I would a painting I wasn't sure I understood.

"Life's more fun when it's a little unexpected," I said lightly, even though my pulse was hammering loud enough to drown out the music.

Claire appeared at my elbow with a fresh drink for Charlie.

I took the cue.

One last glance at the man across from me—quiet, sharp, unreadable—and I turned away.

But as I moved through the room, something in me stayed behind.

And that was the part that worried me.

Chapter Two

DEAN

I should've walked away the second I shook her hand.

A polite nod. A thank-you-for-your-time. A quick, professional exit.

That's what I should have done.

Instead, I stood there like an idiot while the world shrank to the woman before me.

Vivian Thorne.

Owner of the Velvet Room. Star of the show.

And absolutely the last woman I had any business looking at like that.

She was... luminous.

Not flashy. Not cheap.

Just vibrant.

She smiled at me—smooth, practiced—and I knew it wasn't real.

Not entirely.

But there was something under it. Something real enough to make my chest ache.

"Life's more fun when it's a little unexpected," she'd said.

Christ.

I told myself it was just adrenaline. Just the absurdity of the situation—meeting a client in a damn burlesque club, surrounded by velvet and music, and a woman who made every part of me feel ten years younger and twice as stupid.

I knew it wasn't just curiosity. Whatever this was—whatever had just passed between us—was the kind of thing I'd spent years avoiding. And yet, as she turned away without a word, disappearing into the room like smoke through a keyhole, I sat there, restless—like something had started that I wasn't ready to let end.

Charlie clapped a hand on my shoulder. "She's something, huh?"

I didn't answer.

Because *something* didn't even begin to cover it.

***

I stared at the case file on my desk, willing it to offer some justification—any thread I could pull to make this about work.

It didn't.

Charlie's divorce was clean. No contested assets. No custody fight. Just paperwork and deadlines.

Nothing in the file required a conversation with Vivian Thorne.

And yet—

His habits were relevant. Character mattered.

Professional due diligence.

That was the story I told myself.

But the truth was more straightforward. I just wanted to see her again.

I wasn't a fool. I knew what I was doing.

It wasn't about the case.

It was the way something in me tightened when she smiled.

The way my chest locked up when she walked away.

Every reasonable instinct said to leave it alone.

But my hand was already reaching for the phone.

I could keep it professional.

A few questions. A polite follow-up. Just enough to justify the call.

The line rang once. Twice. Three times.

By the fourth, I almost hung up.

And then her voice slid through the speaker—smooth, amused, unhurried. *"The Velvet Room, this is Vivian."*

I automatically sat up straighter, even though she couldn't see me.

"Ms. Thorne, this is Dean Thatcher. We met briefly yesterday through Charlie..." God, I sounded stiff. I forced myself to breathe. "I'd like to schedule a meeting. To discuss a few matters relevant to his case."

"Relevant to his case," she repeated, voice edged with something I couldn't quite name.

"Yes," I said, keeping my voice even. "At my office. Tomorrow afternoon, if you're available."

I gripped the phone tighter, half-waiting for her to laugh. To call me on the lie we were both pretending not to see.

Instead, she said, "Text me the time and address," and gave me her number.

Professional. Efficient. Unbothered.

The exact opposite of how I felt the second the call ended.

I stared at the phone for a full minute, half expecting it to call me an idiot.

Seeing her again was a mistake.

Wanting her, that was reckless.

But I didn't call off the meeting.

Instead, I opened my calendar—and locked the damn thing in.

VIVIAN

The second I ended the call, I just stood there.

Phone still in my hand. Heart doing something stupid and fluttery behind my ribs.

The memory of how he'd looked at me—like I wasn't a fantasy on a stage but something more— had my pulse tapping out a different story—one where a man actually looked *past* the red lips and stage lights.

I wasn't the type to get flustered.

Not by men.

Not anymore.

And yet—

I stared at the phone like it had personally betrayed me.

"Get it together," I muttered under my breath.

Still feeling too jumpy, I did what any sensible woman would do: I called Veronica. My twin was the only person who could usually read me without translation.

She picked up on the second ring.

"What's wrong?"

"Why do you assume something's wrong?"

"Because you don't call in the middle of the day unless you're spiraling or plotting revenge. Which is it?"

I flopped into the nearest chair, pressing the heel of my hand to my forehead.

"I just got summoned to a lawyer's office."

"What did you do now?" she said, sharp and suspicious. Typical Veronica.

I rolled my eyes. "Why do you always assume I'm at fault?"

"Because you usually are."

"Rude," I muttered.

"Accurate," she said, not even pretending otherwise.

I sighed dramatically. "Knew I should've called one of the other sisters."

Veronica laughed. "Oh please. Lola would tell you to punch him, and Eliza would bake him cupcakes."

I dragged a hand through my hair. "It's not like that. I'm not being sued, indicted, or otherwise scandalized."

"Then why the summons, Viv?"

"I'm just answering a few questions," I said, aiming for breezy and landing somewhere closer to *suspiciously defensive*. "Charlie's lawyer wants some context about the club."

Veronica didn't answer right away. When she did, her voice was sharp as a scalpel. "What aren't you telling me?"

I picked at a loose thread on my sleeve. "Nothing."

"Viv." The twin-voice. The one you didn't lie to without consequences.

I sighed. "Fine. Maybe he's...a little hot."

A scandalized gasp. "Vivian Thorne, are you actually admitting attraction? Someone alert the media!"

I rolled my eyes so hard it hurt. "I didn't admit anything."

"Oh, please. You're practically fanning yourself through the phone."

"I am not."

"You are. And you're *smiling*. You never smile after a summons unless it involves petty revenge."

I groaned. "It's professional, Veronica."

Veronica's voice turned downright gleeful. "Oh, you're doomed. Completely and utterly doomed."

"God, I hate you," I grumbled.

"You love me. I'm the only one who tells you the truth."

I muttered something colorful under my breath.

"Call me after," she said. "And don't agree to anything shady without a witness."

"Love you too, Mom," I teased, ending the call.

But the second the line went dead, the calm I'd faked started to fray.

I stood, straightened my spine, and exhaled.

Tomorrow, I'd walk into that office like I owned the damn building—sharp, calm, and unshakable.

***

The dress said control.

The heels said don't underestimate me.

The lipstick said I dare you to look away.

None of it was subtle.

That was the point.

If I was going to pretend this was business, I was damn well going to do it looking like a woman no man could rattle—even if one already had.

I pushed through the heavy glass door, every click of my heels on the polished floor a reminder: Control the room before it controls you.

The receptionist glanced up, her polite smile flickering at the sight of me. I didn't blame her. Their typical clientele probably didn't show up in tailored red dresses and stilettos sharp enough to draw blood.

"Vivian Thorne," I said smoothly. "I have an appointment with Dean Thatcher."

Her fingers fluttered over the keyboard. "He's expecting you. Last door on the left."

I smiled—sharp, polished—and headed down the hall.

One breath.

Two.

Then I stepped into Dean's office like I hadn't already lost sleep over a man I'd barely even touched.

Chapter Three

DEAN

Halfway through reviewing Charlie's financial dis-
closures, I heard the click of heels in the hallway.

Sharp. Even. Unhurried.

I told myself it wasn't her.

But the lie didn't hold long.

When she stepped into the doorway, my focus scattered.

Vivian Thorne.

She didn't just enter the room—she took possession of
it.

Back straight. Chin high. Every detail deliberate.

A woman who understood precisely what kind of attention she could command and never once apologized for it.

I stood automatically because there was no universe where you stayed seated when she was in the room.

"Ms. Thorne," I said, my voice steadier than I felt. "Thank you for coming."

She smiled—slow, lethal, a warning wrapped in satin.

"Pleasure's mine, Counselor." The words purred from her lips.

It hit harder than it should've.

Pleasure.

One word.

That's all it took.

The sound of it curled around my ribs, dragged heat low in my gut—steady, sure, inevitable.

I shouldn't have been thinking about her mouth. How it would feel against mine. Or how those lips could shape other words—lower, rougher, against my skin.

I forced my hands still against the desk. Clenched my jaw so hard it hurt. Tethered myself to the fact that this was a meeting.

Not a surrender.

Because if I let myself feel it—really feel it—I knew I wouldn't stop.

One word, one look, and I was already losing ground.

And the worst part? I wasn't sure I wanted it back.

I motioned to the chair across from my desk. "Please. Have a seat."

She arched one perfect brow—wry, unreadable—but sat and crossed her legs with deliberate ease. The slit of her dress eased open just enough to expose a stretch of thigh that short-circuited every rational thought I had.

I looked away too fast reaching for a file like it might anchor me to something solid. Paper. Ink. Facts. Anything that wasn't her.

"You've known Mr. Halpern for…?" I asked, grateful my voice stayed steady.

Vivian folded her hands lightly in her lap, entirely composed. "A few years. He's a regular."

"At your club," I said, eyes dropping to the notes again.

"No, the knitting circle. Yes, the club."

Deadpan. Dry. A flicker of humor that almost made me smile.

I nodded, forcing myself to stay on task. "Has he ever brought a companion? A date?"

"Once or twice," she said. "Mostly, he comes alone. Orders the same drink. Tips in fives. Predictable, if nothing else."

I scribbled that down. "Any history of temper?"

"Not once."

"Inappropriate? Disrespectful?"

Her lips quirked. "He once complained the velvet upholstery made his pants too warm."

I glanced up despite myself. "That's not quite what I meant."

She smiled a glint of mischief in her eyes. "That's all you're getting."

"Any concerns you'd want on record?"

Vivian tilted her head, amused. "Are we still talking about Charlie?"

My jaw ticked. "Trying to."

Her smile faded into something more careful. Softer.

"Why does it matter what I think?" she asked quietly. "You already know what you're going to say in court."

I paused.

Because she wasn't wrong. But the way she said it made something tighten low in my gut.

"I like having all the pieces before I build my argument," I said. "I don't assume."

She held my gaze. Steady. Unflinching.

"That's rare," she said.

The words shouldn't have landed the way they did. But they did.

I leaned back slightly, suddenly aware of my tight grip on the file.

"Anything else I should know about Mr. Halpern?" I asked, my voice more ragged than I liked.

Vivian studied me—really studied me—before speaking.

"Only that he seems...lonely," she said softly. "Not like he's chasing anything. Just... like someone who's gotten used to being alone—even when it's not what they want."

The words slid under my skin.

"You ever think some people choose it?" I asked, surprising myself. "Loneliness. Because it hurts less than the alternative."

"Yeah." She didn't smile. Didn't flinch. "I think about that more than I should."

I cleared my throat. Snapped the file shut like it would snap my control back into place.

Newsflash: It didn't.

"Thank you for your time," I said, even though I hadn't asked half the questions I meant to.

Vivian stood, graceful and lethal, like she knew I'd still feel the impact long after she was gone.

I stood too—reflex, instinct—and rounded the desk to walk her to the door.

Professional.

Or so I told myself.

We walked side by side—a few feet, no more—but the air between us felt thick enough to drown in.

Her perfume—rich, clean, something I couldn't name—wrapped around me.

She passed close—her dress brushing my leg in a whisper of fabric.

My hand lifted without thinking, fingers pausing just shy of her back.

I stopped myself.

Barely.

I didn't touch her.

But God, I wanted to.

I ushered her out the door instead, muscles tight with restraint.

She glanced back at me, a slow, knowing smile curving her mouth. "Try not to overthink it, Counselor."

And then she was gone.

Leaving me standing there, wondering if she'd meant the case—or something else.

VIVIAN

I made it to the sidewalk before I exhaled.

One foot in front of the other, heels clicking like punctuation in a sentence I wasn't sure how to finish.

What the hell was that?

He hadn't touched me. Hadn't flirted. Hadn't done anything remotely inappropriate.

And still—he'd gotten under my skin more than I cared to admit.

Dean Thatcher was polite. Measured. All that controlled energy behind crisp shirts and sharp lines and a voice that should've come with a warning label. And when he looked at me—really looked—I didn't feel like a performer or a businesswoman or a fantasy in silk and sequins.

I felt seen.

Which was so much worse.

The moment I crossed the street, I yanked my phone from my purse and texted Veronica:

Vivian: *You were right.*

Veronica: *Obviously. About what?*

Vivian: *He's dangerous.*

Veronica: *Did he try anything?*

Vivian: *No. That's the problem. He didn't have to.*

I shoved my phone away before she could reply and turned the corner toward the Velvet Room. Familiar ground. My world. My rules.

Dean Thatcher was sharp and steady and utterly inconvenient.

And if I had any sense left in my head, I'd forget how his eyes lingered like he wanted to memorize me.

***

I returned to the Velvet Room just as Claire was restocking the bar for the evening show.

She glanced over. "You live."

"Don't sound so surprised."

She smirked. "Did the lawyer breathe fire or smolder quietly while trying not to stare at your legs?"

I slid onto one of the high stools. "Bit of both."

Claire raised a brow, poured sparkling water into a crystal glass, and slid it toward me. "You gonna tell me what that was about?"

"Charlie's divorce." I sipped. "Apparently, I'm a character witness now."

Claire folded a bar towel in half. "And?"

"And nothing. It was professional."

Claire tilted her head. "Then why the frown? Wasn't he just another Suit?"

I shook my head, the words scraping out before I could stop them. "That's the problem. He didn't feel like just another anything."

I stared into my glass for a second. Gathering my thoughts felt like herding cats.

"He wasn't what I expected," I said finally. "He looked at me like he couldn't decide if I was dangerous... or damaged."

"And which are you?" she asked.

I smiled without humor. "Depends on the man."

She let the silence stretch, giving me room to say more—or lie.

"You're not used to attention like that," she said after a beat.

I huffed a quiet laugh. "I'm used to all kinds of attention. Just not the kind that feels like it might stick."

Claire said nothing. Just kept polishing.

I set my drink down harder than necessary. "I've seen men like him. Polished. Controlled. They pick women who look good on their arm—and trade them in when the next shiny thing comes along."

Claire looked up, her gaze steady. "You really believe that?"

I shrugged, mouth tight. "I watched my father leave my mother for someone half her age. I watched my mother pretend it didn't hollow her out."

Claire's voice softened. "Maybe not every man is your father."

"Maybe," I said, picking up my glass again. "But I'm not interested in finding out the hard way."

Claire didn't argue. Just raised a brow and slipped away, sensing I'd said as much as I was going to.

I stayed where I was, drink in hand, trying not to replay the look in Dean Thatcher's eyes.

Then I glanced at my phone. My thumb hovered over Lola's name.

I'd already called Veronica.

Which meant I was either spiraling—or certifiably insane—because now I was calling Lola.

Not that she wasn't capable—she was. But I didn't usually do vulnerable.

Especially not with the sister whose version of emotional support involved tequila or tattoos or both.

Still, I hit dial.

She picked up on the second ring. "Viv? Everything okay?"

"Are you busy?"

Lola laughed faintly after a pause. "Well, Tanner's trying to cook. So technically, yes, but only because I might need to extinguish a fire."

I hesitated. Then, against my better judgment, I asked, "Do you think men can be trusted?"

Lola made a sound somewhere between a laugh and a wince. "Heavy question for a Tuesday, Viv."

I grimaced. "Forget I asked."

God, what was I doing? I didn't ask questions like that.

"No, wait—" she cut in, voice softer now. "Didn't expect that one from you, that's all."

I huffed out a breath. "Yeah, well. Desperate times and all that jazz."

She didn't answer right away.

Then, "I didn't used to think they could be trusted. Not after everything. Not really."

I stayed silent, pressing my thumb harder against the glass.

"Then Tanner showed up and didn't treat me like I was broken. He saw the whole damn mess—and didn't flinch."

I closed my eyes against the ache creeping up my chest. "You think that's common?"

"No," Lola said. "That's what makes it worth it."

I exhaled slowly, the knot tightening anyway. "I just... I met someone who didn't flinch. Who didn't leer, push, or try to pretend I was something I'm not. And I don't know if that makes him honest—or dangerous."

Lola didn't answer right away, but when she did, her voice was low but certain. "Sometimes it's both. And sometimes... that's what makes it real."

I sat there, my phone warm against my ear, my heart heavier than it should've been.

"Yeah," I said softly. "That's what I'm afraid of."

Chapter Four

DEAN

I'd made it exactly thirty-six hours.

Thirty-six hours of telling myself she was a distraction.

That I had a job to do. A carefully balanced life. And no business chasing a woman who made my pulse forget how to behave.

I buried myself in motions, filings, case law—anything to keep my hands busy and my mind off the way her voice had wrapped around the word *pleasure* like a velvet noose.

It didn't work.

By noon, I was supposed to be drafting a motion for continuance.

Instead, I sat at my desk, staring at the same paragraph for ten minutes and thinking about a woman I had no business wanting.

By two, I gave up pretending.

It wasn't about Charlie. It wasn't about the case.

But I'd already made peace with the lie I would tell.

I just needed to see her again.

Professional inquiry. Follow-up questions.

That was the story I'd stick to.

I picked up the phone.

Her voice slid through the line—low, smooth, dangerous.

"Vivian Thorne."

My hand clenched around the receiver like it might keep me steady.

"Ms. Thorne. Dean Thatcher. I—uh—had a few follow-up questions regarding Charlie's case."

"Oh really?" she asked, amusement coloring every syllable.

Professional, I reminded myself. *Keep it professional.*

"I was wondering if you might be willing to meet again. Somewhere a little less... formal."

I could practically hear her smirk.

"Less formal?" she said lightly. "Counselor, are you asking me on a date?"

My brain short-circuited for a second.

"No," I said too quickly. Then, forcing my voice into something vaguely calm, "Of course not. Strictly business."

"Mmm," she said, not even pretending to believe it.

"There's a diner a few blocks from my office," I added, clearing my throat. "Billy's. Neutral ground. Public place."

"Neutral ground," she echoed, laughing low—a sound that wasn't helping my cause *at all*.

"Is that lawyer-speak for 'I'm afraid you'll eat me alive'?"

"No, I— That's not what—"

"Relax, Counselor," she teased. "I'll behave. Probably."

Probably.

I ran a hand down my face.

"Three o'clock?" I asked, barely recognizing my own voice.

"I'll be there," she promised.

And then she hung up—leaving me staring at the phone like a man who had just volunteered for execution and couldn't wait for it.

***

I stepped inside Billy's Diner, and the kid behind the counter looked at me as if I'd wandered into the wrong movie set.

And maybe I had.

I headed for a booth in the back, sitting stiffly, the leather squeaking under me.

It wasn't until I settled in that I realized how out of place I looked.

Crisp suit. Perfect knot. The exact right amount of starch in my collar.

Dressing like this was automatic. A reflex. A habit.

But sitting there, under the buzz of neon lights and the smell of burnt coffee, it hit me:

The suit wasn't for the diner. Hell, it wasn't even for Vivian. It was armor. A habit. A shield.

Something I put on every day so no one could see what was underneath. And somewhere along the line, I'd stopped noticing its weight.

Until her.

I loosened my tie just a fraction. Shrugged off my suit coat. Rolled up my sleeves like it might make me look less like a stereotype—and more like a man.

I was still convincing myself I had this under control when the door chimed, and she walked in.

Vivian Thorne didn't belong in Billy's Diner any more than I did—but she made it look deliberate. Like she decided what belonged, not the other way around.

She wore jeans and a simple black top—nothing flashy, nothing calculated.

And still, my world tilted on its axis.

She spotted me and headed over with a walk that should've been illegal—smooth, confident, more than a little dangerous.

I stood as she reached the table because manners were the only thing I still remembered how to do.

"Counselor," she said, amusement sparking in her eyes as she slid into the booth across from me.

"Vivian," I said, and if my voice was rougher than it should've been—well, there were limits to what a man could control.

"This town must be running low on meeting rooms if you're stuck holding court here."

I gave a dry smile. "I thought it might be less intimidating than summoning you back to my lair."

She laughed, low and warm, and something in my chest pulled tight.

"You'd have to work a lot harder to intimidate me, Counselor," she said, flashing a smile sharp enough to cut.

I sat down slowly, feeling every inch too polished for the setting.

She shifted, crossing one leg over the other—and her ankle brushed mine under the table.

A flash of contact. Barely there. But enough to light up every nerve ending I had.

It could've been nothing. A mistake.

But some reckless part of me wanted to believe that it wasn't.

Wanted to believe that she felt it, too.

VIVIAN

I saw it the second my ankle brushed him under the table—accidentally, *maybe*.

That flicker in his eyes.

Like control was something he clutched with both hands—and I'd just loosened his grip without even trying.

I leaned back, letting the moment stretch.

Weighing him.

Then, I decided I was done letting him call the shots.

"Alright, Counselor," I said, voice easy, words anything but. "Enough polite small talk. What's this really about?"

"I told you," he said carefully. "Context for the case."

I lifted a brow. "I call BS. You already have context. Charlie's predictable. Harmless. You didn't drag me to a diner to hear me repeat that."

He didn't argue. Didn't reach for some slick excuse. Just sat there, staring at me like he didn't know how to put it into words.

"I just…" He exhaled. "I wanted to see you again."

The way he said it sent a shiver down my spine, and something twisted low in my stomach.

I felt that old instinct rise—the one that said *don't let it get close*.

Usually, I listened. Usually, I moved first.

This time, I didn't.

Instead, I smiled. "Next time, Counselor, you can just ask."

Then—because it was safer than whatever was burning between us—I added, "But if we're doing lunch, you're buying."

Dean's mouth twitched like he wanted to smile. Instead, he reached for a laminated menu tucked behind the napkin holder.

"Anything you want," he said, voice steady.

I took the menu, pretending to study it. Giving us both a second to breathe.

But the air between us didn't lighten. It thickened.

"So," I said, flipping a page. "Tell me something, Counselor."

He lifted a brow. "Like what?"

I shrugged. "Something real. Not court-approved. Not practiced."

I could almost see the battle behind his eyes—the urge to dodge it, to keep things professional.

But then he said, almost like he didn't mean to, "I thought being a divorce attorney would be about helping people."

I blinked.

That... wasn't what I expected.

He leaned back, eyes fixed on the chipped table between us.

"Figured I'd be the calm in the storm," he said. "The one helping people find a way through the wreckage."

A humorless smile pulled at his mouth.

"Mostly, it's just stepping between two people who would rather set each other on fire than settle anything. Feels less like helping and more like trying to keep two angry rhinos from charging."

The words came out rough—quiet, almost like they surprised him.

Maybe that was what cracked something loose inside me.

Before I could stop myself, I said, "I can't stand happy endings."

His brow furrowed slightly.

I forced a laugh, low and dry. "Movies. Books. Anything tied up with a neat bow. It makes me itchy. Like I'm just waiting for the other shoe to drop."

I shook my head once. "Real life doesn't do bows. It rips the wrapping paper, forgets the card... sometimes lights the whole damn thing on fire."

The words hung between us—too raw, too honest, too much.

Dean nodded. Once. Like he understood more than he should.

The air stretched tight, humming with something dangerous.

So, I did what I always did when things got too real.

I flashed a smile and said, "Well, look at us. Two cynics getting maudlin over diner food."

Dean huffed a breath that might've been a laugh. "Terrifying."

"Terrifying, indeed," I agreed, lifting my glass in a mock toast. "Next thing you know, we'll be writing bad poetry and blaming our parents."

That earned a genuine smile from him—slow, deliberate, and far too devastating.

I told myself the moment passed.

The banter had done its job, smoothing the edges back into place.

But underneath it, the pull didn't fade. It just waited—unspoken, undeniable, inevitable.

Chapter Five

VIVIAN

I set my water glass down and leaned back, letting the tension in the air settle.

"Well," I said, letting the word stretch, playful and sharp, "for a man who claims he's a professional, you're doing a terrible job keeping this interview on track."

Dean's mouth twitched. "You're not exactly making it easy."

I tilted my head, letting my gaze drag over him. Clean lines. Coiled tension. That stubborn, careful control he wore like armor.

"Maybe you're just out of practice."

His eyes darkened, the muscle in his jaw ticking once.

God, it was so easy to get under his skin. Too easy.

Which meant it was time to go—*before* I did something reckless.

I stood, smoothing a hand over the curve of my top. His gaze dropped—quick, automatic, hungry—hitting me like a live wire. Right through the skin. Straight to the parts of me that still remembered what it felt like to be seen—and wanted.

I smiled, slow and sure. "Thanks for lunch, Counselor."

He stood too—because, of course, he did—always the gentleman, even when drowning.

I paused—briefly—close enough to smell his cologne. Something clean and devastating.

I tipped my face up, close enough for him to feel the heat of my breath.

"Maybe next time," I murmured, voice low and wicked, "you'll ask for what you really want."

I let the words hang there—heavy, electric—before turning away with a wicked little smile.

I didn't look back.

I didn't have to.

I could feel him standing there. Still burning.

DEAN

I stood there like a man who'd forgotten how to move.

Vivian Thorne walked out of that diner like she hadn't just knocked the ground out from under me with ten words and a smile.

Maybe next time you'll ask for what you really want.

Christ.

I raked a hand through my hair, forcing myself to sit back down before I did something stupid. Like chase after her. Like kiss her how I'd wanted to from the moment she smiled at me like she already knew how this ended.

I stared at the half-empty water glass she had left behind. Evidence. Proof she'd been here—and I was already losing the war I hadn't meant to start.

This wasn't how it worked. I was supposed to be in control, careful, and one step ahead.

Not this spiraling heat. Not this gut-deep certainty that if I wasn't careful, I'd rewrite every rule I lived by just to stay close to her.

I should've walked away after the first meeting. Filed the paperwork. Filed her under complications to avoid at all costs.

Instead, I was sitting there like a damn fool, still smelling her perfume and wishing I'd asked for what I really wanted.

Her.

Not as a witness. Not as a character reference. Not as another line in a case file.

Just *her*.

And maybe I wasn't ready.

But no way in hell I was going to walk away without a fight.

Chapter Six

VIVIAN

I had *not* spent the last three days thinking about Dean Thatcher.

Not about how he leaned across the table like he wanted to memorize how I breathed. Not about the way he said my name like it was something sacred. Definitely not about the way he loosened his tie—just enough to make me wonder what else might come undone if I applied the right pressure.

No, I'd been busy. Running a club. Managing rehearsals. Pretending I didn't check my phone like an idiot every time it buzzed.

Which made it all the more cruel when fate threw him straight into my path without warning.

Briar Hill's Annual Community Charity Drive. A fundraiser for the local food bank. A reminder that sometimes this town still had its heart exactly where it should be.

I was roped into it by Eliza, who weaponized her dimples and homemade cookies until I caved.

I didn't even like daytime events. There was too much sunlight and too many people pretending they didn't want to one-up each other with baked goods and raffle prizes.

I was standing there, politely pretending to listen to a woman explain her gluten-free scone strategy, when the crowd shifted—and I saw him.

Dean.

Not in a suit.

My brain went haywire for a solid five seconds.

Dark jeans. A soft gray T-shirt that clung in ways it had no business clinging. Sunglasses pushed up into his hair. One hand casually hooked into his pocket like he wasn't the most devastating thing the community center had ever seen.

And because life had a vicious sense of humor, he spotted me almost immediately.

I straightened instinctively, smoothing invisible wrinkles from my sundress, cursing the part of me that felt too seen.

His gaze dragged over me, slow and deliberate, before a half-smile curved at the corner of his mouth—like he knew exactly what he was doing.

And damn him, it worked.

I felt the pull in every nerve ending, low and insistent.

He started toward me, and something quiet unspooled in my chest.

I didn't move. Didn't let it show.

But I felt it.

Whatever this was—it wasn't innocent.

And I couldn't remember the last time I'd wanted to touch danger so badly.

And then he was there—close enough for his scent to catch me off guard. Clean. Subtle. And far too compelling.

I tipped my head back to meet his gaze and let one brow arch slowly. "Well, well. Counselor Thatcher. Look at you—tie off, jaw unclenched. I'm impressed."

"Didn't realize the tie was such a defining feature," he said, voice low and rough.

I shrugged, pretending the sound of it didn't brush right over every exposed nerve. "It was either the tie or the permanent state of mild disapproval."

He chuckled, and damn if the sound didn't punch straight through the fragile armor I'd barely managed to tape together.

"Don't worry," he said. "I can still disapprove without the tie."

I leaned in slightly, letting my voice drop into a purr. "You disapprove of me, Counselor?"

His gaze dropped—just for a second—to my mouth. When he met my eyes again, there was heat banked so deep it made me feel reckless.

"Only when I'm trying to keep my sanity," he murmured.

I smiled sweetly. "Good luck with that."

Dean's answering smile was nothing short of lethal.

Before we could say something truly regrettable, Eliza appeared, weaving through the crowd with panic written all over her sweet, wide-eyed face.

"Viv!" she gasped, clutching a clipboard to her chest like a life raft. "Thank God. I need a huge favor."

I blinked. "Eliza, what—"

"I forgot the donation baskets!" she blurted, cheeks flaming. "They're still at my apartment. I can't leave, and we need them before the auction starts—"

"I'll go," I said automatically because that's what you did for Eliza.

She nodded gratefully. "They're boxed up, but...they won't fit in your car."

I stilled. Of course they wouldn't. My two-seater wasn't exactly known for its cargo capacity.

A voice rumbled beside me before I could even open my mouth to suggest a solution.

"I've got a truck," Dean said casually. "I'll drive you."

I turned to look at him. He met my gaze without flinching. No smirk. No teasing.

"You're sure?" I asked, aiming for cool and probably missing by a mile.

He shrugged one broad shoulder. "Community spirit, right?"

Eliza beamed like a golden retriever who'd just been offered a lifetime supply of biscuits. "You're a lifesaver! Both of you!"

Dean smiled politely, but his eyes never left mine.

I got the feeling community spirit had very little to do with it.

I exhaled and nodded. "Alright, Counselor. Let's go save the day."

DEAN

The second she slid into the truck, the air changed.

Vivian Thorne, in my passenger seat, all soft perfume and sharper edges, wearing a smile that should've come with a warning label.

I gripped the wheel tighter than necessary and pulled onto the road, trying not to notice the flash of bare skin every time the truck jolted over a bump.

Trying not to imagine things I had no business imagining.

We had maybe ten minutes until we hit her sister's apartment.

Ten minutes to sit next to her and pretend my mind wasn't in a back alley brawl with my better judgment.

I stared straight ahead. Counted the seconds. Reminded myself that I was a grown man. A professional. Not some hormone-drunk teenager looking for an excuse to pull over and—

I cut that thought off with a sharp breath.

Jesus.

When was the last time anything made me feel like this? Like I wanted to pull her onto my lap and lose myself in the kind of need I didn't have words for.

"Something wrong, Counselor?" she asked, voice silky—like she already knew the answer.

I cleared my throat. "All good. Just driving."

"Uh-huh." She turned to the window, but not before I caught the smirk tugging at her mouth.

God help me, she was enjoying this. Enjoying unraveling me.

I pulled into the parking lot with a little more force than necessary, gravel crunching under the tires. I hesitated before getting out of the truck, trying to control my heated thoughts.

"You coming, Counselor?" she asked, sliding a slow glance my way—mock innocence sharpened to a blade.

I opened my door like it might save me. Spoiler alert: it didn't.

"Third-floor walk-up," she said, cocking her head. "Think you're up for it, Counselor?"

I bit back a smile. "I can handle it."

Her grin turned wicked. "We'll see." She pivoted and started up the stairs without another word.

I didn't hesitate. Just followed—because stopping? That ship had sailed.

She stepped into the apartment, and I followed close behind, the door clicking shut just as she abruptly stopped. And I walked right into her.

My hands caught her hips before I could stop them.

Just meant to steady her.

But then she turned—

Eyes wide, lips parted—

And I didn't think—I just kissed her like she was the one thing that could save me from going under.

She made a low, startled sound against my mouth—and then her hands were in my hair, on my shoulders, dragging me closer until there was no space between us.

I braced her against the wall, my hand slipping under the hem of her dress, the heat of her skin burning through every shred of control I had left.

She arched into me, breathless, reckless, and I forgot there was a world beyond this moment.

"Dean," she gasped—my name like a plea she didn't mean to speak aloud.

And between that and the kiss, I didn't stand a chance.

And God help me, I wanted all of her.

I kissed her again—deeper, rougher—because words no longer stood a chance.

Not when everything real, everything that mattered, was already right here between us.

Chapter Seven

VIVIAN

I pulled back, breathless and shaking, and Dean's eyes—God, his eyes—were dark with something that scared me to death and made me want it all at once.

"This isn't—" I started, barely recognizing my voice. "I don't usually—"

His hand stayed tangled in my hair, gentler now but no less devastating.

"Me either," he said, the heat in his tone unmistakable. "But goddamn, Vivian—I've never wanted someone as much as I want you."

And how he said my name—like he'd been waiting a lifetime to say it—made me forget why I'd ever considered stopping.

His mouth crashed into mine again, hungry and urgent.

This time, I didn't hold back. This time, I let myself feel it—all of it—the way my blood sang and how his hands anchored me like I was the only thing keeping him sane.

My back hit the wall, and Dean's hands were everywhere—my hips, my thighs, my hair—the heat of him wild and consuming. He lifted me effortlessly, and I wrapped my legs around his waist, grinding into his cock through denim and lace, desperate for more, desperate for everything.

The world blurred, its edges dissolving into heat and need. I fisted the hem of his T-shirt, tugging it up, feeling his raw strength beneath my hands—muscle and heat, too much and not enough.

His skin burned against mine as I yanked the shirt over his head, and his mouth was back on me before it even hit the floor.

I gasped when his hand slipped beneath my dress, fingers tracing the edge of my panties—teasing, testing—until I almost begged him for more.

Then he pushed the lace aside and plunged his fingers inside me—deep, sure, relentless.

A cry ripped from my throat.

I clung to him, shuddering, as he moved—slow at first, then harder, deeper, finding a rhythm that sent white-hot pleasure spearing through me.

"So wet," he growled against my neck. "So fucking wet and tight."

His voice broke, and the sound of it shot through me like a jolt. "Jesus, Vivian."

I couldn't think, couldn't speak—just held on as he fucked me with his fingers, pushing me higher with every hard, perfect thrust.

"Dean," I panted, nails digging into his shoulders. "I'm—I can't—"

My head fell back, a gasp tearing from my lips as his thumb found my clit—circling once, twice—and the world exploded.

I came hard, crying out against his mouth, my body arching, every nerve alight.

Dean didn't stop—he drove me through it, relentlessly, mercilessly, until the world blurred, and the only thing left was the fire licking through my veins.

I trembled in his arms, shattered and gasping, my pulse hammering against the warm, solid thud of his chest.

When I could finally think again, I looked up—and found his eyes locked on me.

Dark. Steady.

Dangerous in a way I wasn't sure I could survive.

But I didn't want to survive it.

"Dean," I whispered, voice shaking, "I want you."

A guttural sound tore from his throat—raw, desperate—and then his mouth was on mine again, bruising and hungry.

He shifted us, one hand at the back of my neck, the other reaching blindly for his wallet.

I caught the glint of a condom, the smooth foil flashing between us.

Relief—and hunger—spiked through me.

He ripped the package open fast, efficiently, and with urgency, and I could barely breathe as he shoved his jeans and boxers down in one fluid motion.

His cock sprang free—thick, hard—and the sight of him hit me like a jolt of electricity.

He rolled the condom on with shaking fingers.

Then he was lifting me again, my thighs wrapping tight around him, my back against the wall, and—

He thrust into me in one deep, brutal stroke.

The shock punched the air from my lungs, and my body clenched around him, greedy and desperate.

He filled me—every hard, thick inch of him—and the sensation ripped through me, white-hot and blinding.

I gasped, arching into him, the stretch of him making me feel wild, alive, undone.

Dean gritted out a curse against my neck, his hands bruising on my hips, his control fraying with every pulse of my body around him.

"Vivian," he rasped, pulling back and driving into me again until I forgot everything but the feel of him moving inside me.

I clung to him, nails biting into his shoulders, every thrust another breaking point, every gasp another surrender.

"You feel—god, you feel so fucking good," he growled.

"Dean," I sobbed, tightening around him, every nerve raw and exposed.

I didn't care about control. Didn't care about pride.

I just needed him.

"Harder," I begged, breathless. "Fuck me—faster—deeper—harder."

A broken sound tore from his chest—and then he gave me what I wanted.

He drove into me, wild and desperate and glorious, and I met every thrust, gasping, shaking, burning alive under the force of him.

The pressure built again—hot, coiled, unbearable.

"Vivian—" he choked out, voice breaking. "I'm not—Jesus—"

I kissed him, hard and deep, and shattered around him—blinding heat, brilliant white, my body locking down around him as I came, every part of me breaking open in his arms.

Dean groaned my name against my mouth as he followed me over the edge—one last brutal thrust, one last desperate sound—and then he was spilling into the condom, throbbing inside me, his whole body going taut.

He held me through it, body trembling, breath ragged against my skin.

And when the world finally tilted back into focus, he was still there, holding me like he might never let go.

DEAN

I held on to her like a man afraid to let go. Terrified she'd disappear. Afraid this would all turn into a daydream the second I opened my eyes.

I felt her breath catch, and then she let out a soft laugh, and her lips curled unmistakably against mine.

When I opened my eyes, she was smiling—wild and breathless—her hair tumbling around her shoulders, her body still wrapped around mine.

"Christ," I whispered, leaning in until our foreheads touched, her name slipping out like a prayer. "Vivian."

She kissed me—soft, slow, sure. And I knew, in that heartbeat that I would do anything to see her like this again. To keep her.

Then—

"Oh my god," she gasped, pulling back, laughter and horror flashing in her eyes. "Eliza's going to kill us."

I blinked, still lost in the post-apocalyptic haze of *us*. "What?"

"We're supposed to be getting the donation baskets for the fundraiser!" she said, wriggling out of my arms, breathless and half-scandalized. "We've been gone forever!"

A rough, half-formed laugh escaped me as I reluctantly set her down, my hands lingering longer than they should have.

"We should—"

"Get the baskets," she said, smoothing her dress with shaky hands that mirrored my own.

I nodded because words were hard when my pulse was still pounding and my mind was still a mess.

I watched her pull herself back together, thinking about how she'd shattered apart for me just minutes ago. How I already wanted to undo her all over again.

I stepped back and adjusted my clothes because I'd never let her leave this room without another taste if I didn't.

We found the donation baskets neatly packed in boxes in the closet. Between the two of us, we gathered them all and headed out.

She caught my eye as we headed for the truck, sly and smiling, and I barely managed not to drop the damn boxes.

"We're doing that again," she whispered, voice like velvet and wildfire.

The certainty in it—the promise—nearly broke whatever thread of control I had left.

We barely made it into the truck before she tested my resolve again.

Her hand crept over to my thigh—light, teasing—settling there like a dare.

"Vivian," I muttered, meaning it to sound stern. It didn't. It sounded like want.

The look she gave me was sweet, calculated, and anything but innocent. The corner of her mouth twitched like she dared me to call her on it. "What?"

"You know exactly what."

Her fingers slid higher, slow and deliberate, burning through denim.

I gritted my teeth and kept my eyes on the road.

"I'm just being supportive," she said, voice pure sin.

I bit back a groan as her hand climbed higher, a trail of fire against my thigh.

"Community spirit, right?" she added, humming softly like she wasn't about to undo me right here behind the wheel.

"You are going to kill me," I growled, but hell if I didn't want to let her.

She didn't back off. Just watched me with that wicked, knowing smirk that made me want to pull over and fuck her all over again.

"Careful, Counselor," she purred. "You look a little hot under the collar."

I choked out a laugh, half-strangled, clenching the steering wheel like it might save me.

"You're so goddamn dangerous."

She shifted, her palm tracing slow, torturous circles against my thigh, inching closer to my hardening cock and it was a goddamn miracle we didn't crash into a tree.

I was seconds from forgetting how to breathe when we pulled into the parking lot.

She laughed under her breath, pulling her hand away at the last possible second, her breath warm against my jaw.

"Looks like we made it."

"Barely," I rasped, cutting the engine and exhaling like I hadn't taken a full breath since I touched her.

Her eyes sparkled—mischief, satisfaction—and something softer underneath. Something that made it impossible to remember why this was supposed to be a bad idea.

"Good job, Counselor," she said, giving my thigh one last squeeze for good measure.

"Vivian," I warned—low, desperate—but she just grinned and hopped out of the truck.

I followed, grabbing the boxes with shaking hands, my body still vibrating from the memory of hers.

Eliza spotted us halfway across the lot—relieved, wide-eyed, and more than a little suspicious.

"Where have you been?" she demanded, pointing her clipboard at us like a weapon.

"Traffic," I said, straight-faced, shameless.

She narrowed her eyes like she could smell the lie on me.

Vivian just laughed, rich and careless. "I told him to take the scenic route."

Eliza shook her head, half-exasperated. "Well, you made it. Just in time."

"Never doubted us for a second," Vivian said, flashing me a glance so wicked it should've been illegal.

I tried—and probably failed—not to look too pleased. Or too guilty.

Chapter Eight

VIVIAN

We gave Eliza the boxes, and she flashed a grateful smile before scurrying off to finish organizing the auction items.

I stood there, watching Dean, wondering if he felt as breathless and undone as I did. Wondering if he was thinking about how I'd fallen apart in his arms. Wondering if he wanted more.

The look in his eyes told me everything I needed to know.

"Hey, Counselor," I said, voice low and dangerously casual. "Think you could meet me back at my place? I might need some... legal advice."

His gaze snapped to mine, a slow, wicked smile spreading.

"Legal advice," he repeated, the corner of his mouth twitching. "Is that what we're calling it these days?"

"Mmm," I answered, stepping closer, feeling bold, breathless, ready to break every rule I'd ever made. "Very pressing matters."

I let my fingers brush his—light enough to feel like a promise.

"Urgent, even?" he asked, voice rough, full of heat.

"Possibly life or death."

He chuckled, low and devastating, then leaned in, his breath warm against my ear.

"I'll be there."

***

I got to my apartment just before he did. Long enough to do a quick sweep of the place. Long enough to admit that I was utterly, shamelessly gone.

The second I heard the knock, my pulse sprinted. My skin hummed with memory. And God help me—I ached for him.

I opened the door—and there he was.

Eyes locked on mine. Mouth parted—dangerously close, dangerously sure. And every inch of him dared me not to run.

"Counselor," I said, smiling up at him with too much need, "glad you could make it."

"Vivian," he said—and it was a promise.

He pulled me into him, voice low, breath hot against my skin. "How urgent are we talking?"

He kicked the door shut behind him—and then his mouth was on mine. Hot. Hungry. Devastating.

By the time he pulled away, we were both breathless, clinging.

"Tell me if this is too much," he rasped, his hands cradling my face, searching my eyes. "Tell me if you need me to back off."

I laughed—a wild, broken sound. "Dean. If you back off, I might die."

He groaned—a rough, desperate sound—and kissed me again, fierce and consuming.

Backing me toward the bedroom. Dragging me under all over again.

We barely made it to the mattress.

He stripped my sundress over my head, kissing down the curve of my neck. Every graze of his lips set my skin on fire.

I tugged at his T-shirt, frantic to feel him, finally yanking it over his head and drinking him in—broad shoulders, lean muscle, the kind of body that begged for hands, lips, and reckless decisions.

He watched me shimmy out of my panties, his eyes darkening, his jaw going tight. I hooked my thumbs into his waistband and pulled him down to me—the weight of him grounding, electrifying.

"This time," he murmured against my mouth, "I'm taking my time."

He cupped my breasts, thumbs grazing over my nipples through my bra, and I arched into his touch, aching for more.

He unclasped it with a slow flick of his fingers, and when the lace slipped away, the look in his eyes made me shiver.

He lowered his mouth to my nipple and sucked deeply. Each long, deliberate pull created an intense, aching sensation that ignited sparks in my body and left my pussy drenched with desire.

I tugged at his hair, desperate for more, but he only chuckled—low, wicked.

"Impatient, Vivian?"

"Yes," I gasped, shameless. "God, yes."

He just smiled, dangerous and knowing. Reading me far too well, he caught my wrist when my hand drifted down, desperate for friction.

"Uh-uh," he said, voice a dark caress. "Not yet."

I whimpered—a sound I'd never made before—and he kissed a path lower, lower, every inch of my skin a live wire.

"Patience is overrated," I panted, arching into him.

He only smiled again—and pinned my wrists over my head with one hand. I nearly came undone right then.

He took his time until I was trembling, begging, panting his name.

"Please," I whispered, desperate.

He groaned, voice thick with want. "God, I love the way you say that."

"Then stop teasing—"

His mouth finally reached my core, and the world narrowed down to the exquisite sensation of his lips and tongue, exploring every intimate curve and contour of my pussy.

His tongue moved slowly, deliberately, relentlessly. I bucked against him, gasping, and crying out with every flick, every stroke.

When he slid two fingers inside me—perfect, sure, deep—I broke apart. Shattered. Came so hard that the world turned white around the edges.

He didn't stop until I was whispering his name like a prayer.

I pulled him up to me, kissing him hard—wild and wanting and desperate. His hands were already at his waist, shoving down his pants and boxers in one rough motion. I fumbled blindly for the nightstand, finding the condom by touch.

He groaned when I tore it open, a sound so rough I felt it everywhere.

"Hurry," he begged against my mouth.

I rolled it over him, feeling him thick and hard and trembling with restraint.

Then he thrust into me—deep, sudden—and the shock of it made me cry out, arching against him.

He filled me completely, perfectly, the stretch of him igniting every nerve; every place I'd forgotten could feel this good.

DEAN

It was like the first time—Wild. Consuming. No room to breathe. No room to think.

Only better.

I pulled her closer, my mouth open against her skin, my hands gripping her hips like I might lose my mind if I let go. She moved under me, with me, her body arching, her breath coming in ragged, desperate gasps—and I was already a lost cause. Already so deep inside her, I could barely breathe.

Her legs locked around my waist, and I drove into her, every rough stroke pushing us closer to the edge.

I couldn't stop.

Couldn't hold back.

Couldn't do anything but give in to the wild, reckless rhythm she pulled from me.

She gasped my name—a breathless, broken sound—and I felt her tighten around me, slick and hot and impossibly tight.

The edge slammed into me, rushing up fast and brutal, and I didn't fight it.

"Vivian," I groaned, my voice breaking apart as my body shuddered, feeling every ripple, every tight, wet clench, my vision blurring as I came with a raw, staggering force. Everything else fell away until there was only her—and this.

We stayed tangled until the world finally slid back into focus—until I could see the curve of her mouth, the flush across her skin, and the impossible, breathtaking reality of her.

I eased back carefully, and she let out a low, satisfied sound—a sound that hit me harder than any orgasm ever could.

She smiled—wild and wicked and beautiful—and I knew right then I was absolutely hers.

"We're doing that again," she said—same words, same grin, but this time it wasn't a dare. It was a promise.

A laugh tore out of me—rough, unsteady, real. "Yeah, we are."

Vivian shifted, her hair spilling across the pillow, her body still impossibly close to mine.

"Think you can keep up, Counselor?" she teased, arching a brow.

I met her gaze, steady and unflinching. "You have no idea."

She kissed me—slow and deep—and I felt my body respond before I could catch my breath.

Christ. Again?

I groaned into her mouth, barely hanging onto my sanity.

"Vivian," I muttered, pulling back just enough to breathe, "you're going to be the death of me."

Her fingers trailed down my stomach, feather-light, teasing.

"Looks like you're still alive, Counselor." Her voice was pure velvet—and pure sin. "And just as eager as the first time."

A rough sound escaped me—half disbelief, half desperation—as she wrapped her hand around my cock and started stroking.

She grinned, wicked and unrepentant.

"Unless," she teased, her hand sliding lower, fingers wrapping around my balls, "you need a break?"

I growled low in my throat—and flipped her over onto her stomach.

I dragged her up onto her knees, moving in close behind her, unable to stop myself even if I'd tried.

I didn't know how she made me feel like this—how she made me feel like a twenty-year-old again, hard and aching and ready to lose my damn mind.

I grabbed another condom, tearing it open with shaking hands, barely holding on.

Vivian rubbed back against me—hot, desperate—and I nearly lost it right there.

I groaned and slid the condom on quickly.

She looked over her shoulder, eyes locking with mine—and whatever I thought I knew about control shattered. Because the look in her eyes? It leveled me.

I thrust into her deep and hard—and the jolt of it hit us both.

She cried out—high, needy—and her body clamped down around me again, slick and tight and impossibly good.

I tangled my fingers in her hair, pulling just enough to make her gasp.

God, she was perfect. Wild and desperate and so fucking beautiful I couldn't breathe.

She let out a ragged moan—and I gave up holding anything back.

I drove into her—faster, harder—my body crashing into hers, every thrust pushing us closer to the edge.

"Dean," she gasped, desperate and wild. "Don't—don't stop—"

No chance in hell.

I held on, barely hanging together, feeling her tremble, feeling everything coiling, winding tighter.

One more thrust—

She cried out, her body clenching around me, and I lost it.

I slammed into her deep and hard one last time, letting the orgasm tear through me—wild, brutal, blinding.

We came together—

A riot of sound.

A rush of heat.

A breaking apart so completely I didn't know where she ended, and I began.

We collapsed onto the bed—tangled, shaking.

I eased out of her slowly, carefully, every nerve humming, and pulled her into my arms.

I didn't care that my muscles felt shot. Didn't care that the room was still spinning.

I only cared about the way she smiled up at me.

Chapter Nine

VIVIAN

The sun was just starting to seep through the blinds when I woke.

Dean was still asleep beside me — warm, steady, his arm slung over my waist like he belonged there.

I froze, heart stuttering.

I was sure I looked like a mess. My hair was tangled, my makeup smudged, and I had none of the polish I usually wore like a shield.

This wasn't the version of me men usually wanted.

I slid out of bed carefully, barely breathing, and tiptoed to the bathroom, shutting the door softly.

Staring at my reflection, my stomach twisted.

No armor. No safety net. No curated version of myself to hide behind.

Just... Vivian.

I splashed water on my face, scrubbing away the remnants of the night. Trying—desperately—to find something polished in the mirror. Something he could still want.

When I opened the door, the towel pressed to my face; I wasn't expecting him to be awake.

But he was.

Sitting up against the headboard, sheet slung low across his hips, dark eyes locked on me.

Wide awake.

And seeing everything.

"Morning, beautiful," he said, voice rough with sleep.

I froze.

Because there was no hiding now.

He smiled, slow and steady—like seeing me like this wasn't a shock. Like I didn't need my armor.

I felt the panic rise—fast, brutal—clawing up my throat before I could stop it.

"You don't have to say that," I said, voice tight.

Dean frowned. "Say what?"

"That I'm beautiful."

He blinked, brow furrowing like I'd just spoken a different language. "I'm not saying it because I have to."

His gaze held mine, unflinching. Like the truth had just settled between us, and he wasn't backing down. "Vivian—"

"Don't," I said quietly, the words slipping out as I took a small step back, unable to stop myself.

Confusion flickered across his face, along with hurt.

But the instinct to protect myself slammed into place before I could stop it.

"I have a lot to do today," I said, voice high and bright and false. "You should probably—"

I gestured vaguely toward the door, hating myself more with every word.

He wasn't angry—just quiet, with a sadness in his eyes that made it harder to breathe.

"Okay," he said, voice low and steady. "If that's what you want."

It wasn't. God, it wasn't.

I tightened my grip on the towel, stepped aside, and let him gather his things.

And when the door clicked shut behind him, I finally let myself sink to the floor, pressing my hands to my face—

hating that I'd written the ending I'd feared the most and still felt like I didn't have a choice. Because it always ended the same.

They see the real you.

And then they leave.

***

I sat there, staring at the empty space where Dean had been.

The way the sunlight slanted through the blinds. The rumpled sheets. The fragile pieces of a morning that could've been something different.

If I weren't... me.

If I weren't so good at ruining things before they had the chance to ruin me.

My hand moved without thinking, fumbling for my phone like it might anchor me.

I didn't even realize I'd called Veronica until she answered.

"Viv? What's wrong?"

My throat closed up. I almost hung up. Almost lied.

But something cracked open instead.

"I kicked him out," I said, my voice small and raw.

"Dean?" she said carefully.

I squeezed my eyes shut. "He saw me. All of me. No makeup, no armor. Just... me."

Veronica's voice dropped, softer now. "And?"

"And he didn't run." The words ripped out of me. "I did."

I heard her exhale—slow, steady. "Oh, Viv."

"I couldn't—" My voice broke. I pressed a hand to my forehead. "He said I was beautiful. Like he meant it. And I couldn't believe him. I couldn't... I couldn't let him be the one to leave."

Veronica didn't say anything at first.

When she did, her voice was gentler than I'd ever heard.

"I didn't realize it went that deep for you," she said. "The armor. The needing to be perfect."

I let out a choked sound that wasn't quite a laugh. "It's always been that deep."

"I'm sorry," she said quietly. "I thought... I thought you wore it because you liked it. The polish. The control."

"I do," I whispered. "But it's not just that."

"I know," she said. "I see it now."

Veronica's voice was low but fierce. "You don't need the armor, Viv. You never really did, not with him."

I shook my head, even though she couldn't see me. "He's going to realize I'm not perfect. And he's going to leave."

She laughed—a soft sound that cracked something open in me. "Vivian. He already knows you're not perfect. None of us are. And he stayed anyway."

I closed my eyes, the ache in my chest splintering wide open.

"He's not our father," Veronica said, her voice fierce with conviction. "This isn't *that* story."

I didn't answer. Couldn't.

"Let yourself be loved," she said. "You don't have to be flawless."

The tears spilled over then—silent, furious.

Because some part of me wanted so badly to believe her.

Wanted so badly to believe him.

"I'm scared," I whispered.

"I know," she said, steady as ever. "But maybe that's how you know it's real."

I stayed there on the floor long after we hung up.

Stayed until the light shifted.

Until the apartment grew small around me.

I'd spent so long guarding myself with solitude—telling myself I didn't need more or deserve more.

But the thought of losing him?

That was the first thing that ever made me question the lie.

DEAN

I drove around for a while after leaving her apartment.

No destination. No plan. Just me—and the silence that made it impossible to lie to myself.

I kept replaying it in my head—how she looked when she pushed me away. Not angry. Not cold. Just... scared.

And somehow, that left a deeper mark than anything she could've said.

I should've been angry. I meant every word, every look—and she still didn't trust it. Didn't trust me.

But I wasn't angry. I was hollow. Confused. And still—God help me—certain.

Because what I saw in her eyes wasn't rejection.

It was fear.

And beneath that? Hope. Small. Fragile. Beating like a trapped bird in her chest.

She thought pushing me away would hurt less than letting me stay.

Thought giving me an out would save her from the heartbreak she believed was coming.

Hadn't she realized it yet? I was already all in. Already too far gone.

I gripped the steering wheel tighter, my pulse pounding harder the longer I sat with it.

I didn't know when it had happened. When she got under my skin, into my blood—became the one person I didn't want to live without.

Maybe it was that day at the diner.

Or when she smiled like she dared the world to hurt her.

Or looked at me like she didn't believe in miracles... but was willing to risk it anyway.

It didn't matter when it happened or how. All I knew was that whatever this was between us was real. And real was worth fighting for. I wasn't walking away from her, from this... not even if she tried to give me a hundred reasons to.

She deserved someone who didn't scare easy. Someone who stayed. Someone who could look at every sharp, broken, brilliant part of her and choose her anyway.

And I was damn sure that someone was me.

I flicked my blinker on and made a hard U-turn.

Because this wasn't over. Not by a long shot.

***

I didn't bother texting. Didn't call. I wasn't giving her the chance to close the door before I even knocked.

I just parked, climbed the stairs two at a time, and knocked.

Stillness wrapped around me, but under my skin, everything raced. The air felt tight like it was holding its breath—waiting, just like me. I could almost feel her on the other side of the door, her heartbeat quick, her hand hovering near the handle, deciding whether to let me in or let fear win.

I knocked again. Softer this time.

"Vivian," I said, voice low, steady. "I'm not here to push. Or fight. I'm just... here."

Still nothing.

I scrubbed a hand over my jaw, my heart hammering harder than it had any right to.

"I'm not leaving," I said, leaning my forehead against the door. "Not unless you look me in the eye and tell me this—*us*—meant nothing to you."

The lock clicked, the door eased open—and there she was, stripped of all her armor and still, somehow, the most stunning woman I'd ever seen.

I stepped inside, closing the door softly behind me.

The air between us buzzed with all the things we hadn't said. All the fear. All the wanting. All the hope.

I stayed a few feet back. Gave her room.

"I'm not here to make this harder," I said, voice rough. "I'm here because you're scared. And I'm not."

She opened her mouth—probably to argue or lie—but I shook my head.

"Don't," I said, voice low. "Don't tell me it didn't mean anything. I know fear when I see it, Vivian—but I also know what it feels like when something's real. And this... this is real.

Vivian looked away, her voice barely above a whisper. "I spent a long time thinking I had to be perfect. That if I wasn't... people would leave."

I took a step closer, slow and steady. "I'm not going anywhere."

"You should hate me," she whispered, broken.

"I don't," I said simply.

"You should leave."

"I'm not going anywhere," I repeated.

Her breath hitched. Her eyes shimmered, wide and raw.

"I'm scared," she said so quietly it almost broke me.

I stepped closer. Close enough to reach her if she let me.

"I'm not," I said, my voice catching. "You don't scare me, *this* doesn't scare me."

Her eyes flooded, but she didn't look away.

"I'm not perfect, Vivian," I said, softer now. "You're not either. That's not what this is about."

She stared at me like I was offering her something she didn't know she was allowed to want.

So I said it: "You don't have to be perfect to be loved."

The first tear slipped down her cheek.

Then another.

I closed the distance between us, lifted my hand—slow, careful—and brushed the tears away with my thumb.

She shuddered under the touch but didn't pull back.

"I see you," I said, voice breaking. "All of you. And I'm still right here."

For a long, gut-wrenching moment, she just stared at me.

Then—like she was stepping off the edge of a cliff—she reached for me.

Wrapped her arms around my waist. Buried her face in my chest. And let herself fall.

I caught her. Held her tight.

Tangled my fingers in her hair and breathed her in.

And when she whispered my name against my heart, I knew she wasn't running. And I wasn't letting go.

Epilogue

VIVIAN

6 months later

The Velvet Room had settled into its version of quiet—just the low hum of exit lights, the soft clink of glass behind the bar, and the hush that followed a night of music and noise.

I grabbed my jacket from backstage, already spinning tomorrow's rehearsal schedule through my mind.

Dean was leaning by the door, watching me with that steady, impossible gaze that still made my chest ache in ways I wasn't used to.

"You ready?" he asked, voice low.

"Almost." I slung the jacket over my arm and returned to the bar to grab my keys.

That's when I heard it — the soft creak of the stage stairs.

I looked up, frowning—only to see him climbing the stairs like he belonged there. Like the spotlight didn't faze him. Like this was precisely where he was meant to be.

He stepped into the low pool of light at center stage—no music, no script, just him. Dean was standing there with nerves in his eyes, but his shoulders were squared like he wasn't going anywhere. "I don't have a routine," he said, voice rough with something that hit me square in the chest. "No velvet. No feather. No smoke and mirrors."

I swallowed hard, my heart climbing higher with every word.

"All I've got is this," he said. He held his arms out slightly — open, bare, unguarded. "Me. The guy who's stupidly, hopelessly in love with you."

The world tilted. Tilted and steadied and came into sharper focus than it ever had before.

Dean smiled—quiet, sure, like giving me his heart was the easiest thing he'd ever done. And it took every breath I had not to fall apart.

I did the only thing that made sense. I dropped my jacket, every last fear, every broken story I used to tell myself about love, leaving, and loss, and I ran.

Ran down the aisle, up the stairs, across the stage, straight to him.

Dean met me halfway.

I launched myself into his arms and kissed him hard, fierce, shameless. He caught me like he always had — strong, steady, and sure — and kissed me back like he'd been waiting his whole life for it.

When we finally broke apart, I leaned in, brushing my mouth against his. "Took you long enough, Counselor."

He laughed—soft, low, and so full of love it made my chest ache.

He cupped the back of my neck, his forehead resting against mine.

"I love you," he whispered.

And I believed him.

And I knew I wasn't alone anymore.

Not ever again.

***

Dear Reader,

Thank you so much for reading *Silk & Silence*—and for stepping into the guarded hearts of Vivian and Dean with me.

This story was built on walls: the kind we build to survive, to protect, to keep love at a distance. But it's also about what happens when someone finally sees through the cracks—and chooses to stay.

Vivian's control, Dean's quiet armor, and the slow unraveling of everything they thought they needed to stay safe made this one of the most tender, vulnerable books I've ever written. I hope their journey reminded you that being seen—truly seen—can be the bravest kind of love.

If *Silk & Silence* made you swoon, sigh, or feel a little less alone, I'd be so grateful if you left a review. Every review helps new readers discover the series and supports stories that center flawed, fierce, and deeply human love. You can review the book here.

The Thorne sisters still have stories to tell—and I promise they're just getting started.

With all my love,
Hana York

***

If you loved *Silk & Silence*, you won't want to miss the next book in the Thorne Sisters series: *Pleasure & Prose*.

Pleasure & Prose

She's pure confidence and provocation. He's all restraint and repressed desire. But when opposites combust, even the rules don't stand a chance.

Simon Radcliffe is a buttoned-up British professor teaching at the local university, all nervous smiles and devastatingly proper manners. But when a wrong turn leads him through the doors of Pleasure & Co., he meets Veronica Thorne—a woman who exudes power, mystery, and the kind of sensual self-possession that makes him forget how to breathe.

Veronica doesn't do flustered. And she definitely doesn't go for repressed academics. But there's something about Simon—something curious and unguarded—that makes her pause. And when he asks her to tea—with the stiff sincerity of a man completely out of his depth—she says yes. Against every instinct, she says yes.

What begins as a slow, simmering pull becomes a wildfire neither of them is ready for. And when the past rears its nosy, unwelcome head, they'll have to decide what they're really fighting for.

Pleasure & Prose is a steamy, emotional small-town romance about opposites that ignite, slow burns that explode, and a cinnamon roll hero who learns the right woman doesn't just unravel you—she shows you who you've been all along.

Pleasure & Prose is available on Amazon here. Keep reading for a sneak peak!

Sneak Peak of Pleasure & Prose

Prologue

VERONICA

Pleasure & Co. was steady this afternoon.

I leaned a hip against the counter, arms folded, watching women move through the aisles with easy certainty.

They compared options, read labels, and asked questions without embarrassment.

Toys. Accessories. A few racks of lingerie along the back wall.

Not the heart of the shop, but a nice touch.

People liked to categorize places like mine.

Places where women could be themselves.

Where they could live, love, and learn without shame.

Where they could own their bodies, and their pleasure, without asking permission.

That made some people uncomfortable.

The idea that women didn't need to be told what was acceptable.

That they could want more, take more, *be* more, and not apologize for any of it.

It was easier to pretend this place was reckless.

That the women who came here were desperate. Or broken. Or sad.

Anything to avoid admitting the truth: These women were free.

And they didn't need anyone's approval to stay that way.

The bell above the door chimed.

I looked up, expecting another woman ready to take what she needed without apology.

Instead, a man stood just inside the entrance, looking like he wasn't sure he was allowed to be here.

Tall. Lean. Rumpled brown hair. Tortoise shell glasses.

A tweed jacket that had seen too many dry cleanings.

The kind of man who belonged behind a stack of books, not under the soft glow of Pleasure & Co.'s lights.

Attractive, despite the nerves practically rolling off him.

Maybe even because of them.

He took one wide-eyed look around and stiffened, like he'd just realized he was hopelessly out of place.

Our eyes met.

He straightened his jacket, shoved his hands into his pockets, and started toward the counter with the grim determination of a man walking into traffic.

A slow smile tugged at the corner of my mouth.

My day just got a lot more interesting.

Chapter One

SIMON

I was lost.

Hopelessly, embarrassingly lost.

The directions to Paper Moon Bookshop were still sitting neatly on the bureau at my flat.

I'd been so sure I wouldn't need them.

After all, how hard could it be to find a bookshop in a town this size?

Impossible apparently.

Briar Hill was not laid out sensibly.

Or perhaps it was, and my English instincts refused to cooperate.

Either way, I'd been walking in circles for fifteen minutes and was dangerously close to being late.

I scanned the street for anything that looked remotely bookish.

A florist—closed.

A café—boarded up for renovations.

An antique shop—lights off, sign flipped to *Sorry, We're Closed*.

And then—*Pleasure & Co.*

The only shop open.

The only option.

I stopped dead in my tracks.

Modest gold lettering marked the window, light from within casting a soft gleam across the glass.

Inside, warm hues and velvet displays hinted at a world I had no business stepping into.

Absolutely not the bookshop.

Still... a shop was a shop.

Someone inside might give me directions.

Preferably before I lost what little dignity I had left.

I pushed the door open before I could talk myself out of it.

A soft chime rang above me, and warm air wrapped around my shoulders like a trap.

Velvet displays. Glass cases glowing under low, inviting lights.

And shelves lined with objects I absolutely was not prepared to encounter in public.

I tried not to stare at any item too long, fearing the comparison might not be flattering.

Movement behind the counter caught my eye.

A woman.

She stood with one hip cocked, arms folded across a silky raspberry blouse, watching me with a calm, unreadable expression.

Dark hair tucked behind one ear. Sharp mouth painted a deep berry color.

Poised. Elegant. Entirely unbothered by the absurdity of my presence.

Our eyes met and I forgot, briefly, why I was there at all.

There was nothing shy about her. Nothing hesitant or uncertain.

She seemed entirely comfortable in her skin, something I'd spent most of my life quietly wishing I could be.

The heat rising up the back of my neck had nothing to do with the temperature.

I straightened my jacket, shoved my hands into my pockets, and walked toward her.

She didn't smile.

She just watched, like someone studying a fish out of water.

I had the distinct feeling I was making a memorable first impression.

Words.

I needed words.

Preferably not the ones scrambling through my mind like startled livestock.

"Good afternoon."

Polite. Neutral. Safe.

I opened my mouth and immediately forgot how to be a functioning member of society.

Because of course, only a madman would walk into a shop like this and start with *good afternoon*, as if browsing vibrators and blindfolds were a standard part of one's day.

Brilliant, Radcliffe. Absolutely brilliant.

I cleared my throat, resisting the overwhelming urge to flee.

"Forgive me," I managed, voice a beat too stiff. "I'm terribly sorry to bother you, but I seem to have lost my way."

Lost my way.

In a shop like this.

Outstanding.

It was, by all accounts, not my finest hour.

VERONICA

He wasn't the first man to wander into Pleasure & Co. looking lost.

But he might've been the first who didn't wear his discomfort like a joke.

No smirk. No leering glance.

Just that stiff posture and polite desperation, like he'd rather be anywhere else, and couldn't bring himself to be rude about it.

Interesting. Unexpected.

Most men who walked in here had a confident swagger.

Like the sheer act of crossing the threshold made them bold and entitled.

They saw the window displays, the velvet chairs, the curated toys, and assumed they understood.

But not him.

There was no performance in the way he stood there, fidgeting awkwardly.

No calculation in the way his gaze skated carefully over the displays.

He wasn't pretending to be at ease.

He wasn't pretending at all.

And somehow, that was more magnetic than any polished charm or empty promise had ever been. I kept my expression neutral, resting one hand lightly on the counter.

He shifted slightly, unsure if he was meant to speak or melt into the floor.

I stayed exactly where I was, letting the silence stretch.

If he wanted something, he'd have to find the words himself.

He cleared his throat.

"Forgive me," he said, each word crisp and deliberate.

"I seem to have lost my way. I'm looking for the Paper Moon Bookshop. Would you happen to know where it is?"

His unmistakable English accent made even getting lost sound dignified.

Maybe that explained his stiffness. Or, maybe not.

Either way, it made him even more interesting.

Something about him, something in the way he stood there, all earnest discomfort and ironclad politeness, made me want to see what might be hiding under all that careful restraint.

The pull was instant.

Sharp.

Unavoidable.

I tucked a strand of hair behind my ear and offered the smooth, practiced smile I usually reserved for nervous first-time buyers.

"Two blocks down," I said. "Hang a right at the coffee shop with the green awning. You can't miss it."

Relief flickered across his face.

He nodded, murmured a quiet, "Thank you," and turned to go.

And just like that, I knew I wasn't ready to let him.

"Actually," I said lightly, before he reached the door, "I'm heading that way myself. I've got a delivery for the owner. I'm Veronica Thorne, by the way, owner of Pleasure & Co."

He hesitated, clearly unsure whether he was supposed to accept or if saying yes would somehow violate a rule only he knew.

"Simon Radcliffe," he said, voice polite but uncertain. "I teach at the university."

I tucked another strand of hair behind my ear, letting a small smile curl my mouth.

"Relax," I added, voice low and dry.

"I don't bite, unless asked nicely."

That earned me the smallest huff of laughter.

A warm flicker of satisfaction curled in my chest, sharper than I expected.

God, it had been a long time since teasing someone felt this good.

"I'll just be a second," I said, nodding toward the back.

He gave a short, awkward nod and stayed put.

I slipped through the curtain, grabbed the slim brown package off the shipping shelf, and returned a moment later.

He was exactly where I'd left him, hands in his pockets doing his best not to look at anything too closely.

When he caught sight of me, he straightened.

Flushed, just a little.

Adorable.

Without a word, he stepped aside, falling into step as I crossed the room.

At the door, he moved ahead just enough to reach it first, pulling it open with stiff, careful politeness.

Chivalrous to the bone.

The kind of man who held doors, not to be noticed, but because it was wired into him.

Dangerous, that kind of decency.

The kind that could undo a woman if she wasn't careful.

And I wasn't in the business of being undone.

I stepped past him into the sunlight, the package tucked under my arm, and felt his presence hover close behind me, like he still wasn't sure he belonged at my side.

I wasn't sure either.

But I knew better than to underestimate the pull of curiosity, my kryptonite.

Continue reading *Pleasure & Prose* on Amazon here.

Hana York Books

Hearts on Duty Series

Sparks of Temptation

Love's Anchor

On Call for You

Investigating Desire

Falling for the Rescue

A Heart Worth Mending

***

Falling for the Billionaire Series

Hating Mr. Wentworth

Tempting Mr. Dawson
Unraveling Mr. Ashford

***

The Thorne Sisters Series

Ink & Iron
Silk & Silence
Pleasure & Prose
Lessons & Leather

***

The Men of Hawks Landing
Mountain Made
Mountain Found
Mountain Promise
Mountain Kept

***

For a full list of titles, please visit Hana York's website
www.HanaYork.com

About the Author

Hana York writes fast-paced, heart-pounding contemporary romance packed with irresistible heroes, strong heroines, laugh-out-loud banter, and just the right amount of spice to keep things sizzling. Her books are for readers who love grumpy men falling hard, fierce women who don't need saving, and the kind of chemistry that sparks off the page.

When she's not crafting stories full of love, tension, and toe-curling moments, you'll find her daydreaming about small-town charm, plotting ridiculous meet-cutes, and consuming an unhealthy amount of coffee. She believes in happily-ever-afters, overprotective heroes who don't stand a chance against their heroines, and that every great love story should come with a side of sass.

If you love forced proximity, off-limits attraction, sizzling tension, and romance that makes your heart race, welcome to the world of Hana York!

Follow Hana York for new releases, exclusive content, and behind-the-scenes fun! www.HanaYork.com

Find all her books here: https://www.amazon.com/author/hanayork

Follow her on Instagram: https://www.instagram.com/hanayorkromance/

Follow her on TikTok: https://www.tiktok.com/@hanayorkauthor

Follow her on Facebook: https://www.facebook.com/hanayorkromance/

Follow her on Good Reads: https://www.goodreads.com/author/show/54826946.Hana_York

Join her mailing list here: https://www.hanayork.com/subscribe

More to Read

I f you enjoyed this story, I've got more where that came from! Keep reading for a look at my other books.

Hearts on Duty Series

Sparks of Temptation

A sizzling small-town romance where forced proximity turns up the heat between a stubborn chef and a protective firefighter.

Olivia Harper came to Anchor Bay for a fresh start—not a flirty distraction. After rebuilding her life, she has no time for complications, especially the kind that come with broad shoulders, a cocky grin, and a hero complex.

Jack Lawson knows how to keep his cool under pressure. As a firefighter, protecting people is second nature. But Olivia? She doesn't want rescuing, and she sure as hell doesn't want him getting too close. When a plumbing mishap lands him as her unexpected housemate, their battle of wills turns into something neither of them can ignore.

The problem? Olivia has spent years proving she doesn't need anyone, while Jack's instincts tell him to stand back before he wants something he can't have. But some flames refuse to die out...**A small town full of charm. A slow-burn romance packed with heat. A love story that proves the best things in life are worth the risk.**

***

Love's Anchor

A sizzling small-town romance where years of friendship ignite into something neither of them can ignore.

Brooke Taylor has spent years keeping her feelings for Theo Morgan buried beneath sharp comebacks and stubborn denial. As a no-nonsense cop in Anchor Bay, she's never let emotions get in the way of the job—especially when it comes to the charming, frustrating bar owner who knows exactly how to push her buttons.

Theo has always played it safe when it comes to Brooke. She's his best friend, his steady constant—the one woman he can't afford to lose. But when a break-in at his bar forces them into close quarters, the tension between them finally boils over.

Can they risk their friendship to take a chance on love? Or will fear keep them apart forever?**A small town full of charm. A slow-burn romance packed with heat. A love story where friendship is just the beginning.**

***

On Call for You

He swore she was off-limits. She's ready to prove him wrong.

Dr. Sophie Whitaker has spent her career proving herself in a world that underestimates her. As a brilliant but petite doctor, she's fought for respect every step of the way. Moving back to Anchor Bay is supposed to be a fresh start—not a temptation in the form of Lucas Carter. The rugged EMT with a cocky grin and a hero complex. The man her brother trusts with his life... and the one she should definitely stay away from.

Lucas Carter lives by two rules: stay cool under pressure and never, ever cross the line with Sophie Whitaker. Even if she's gorgeous. Even if she's sharp-witted and impossible to ignore. Even if, after one stormy encounter stranded together, the idea of walking away feels damn near impossible.

Now, every stolen glance and lingering touch has Lucas questioning everything—especially the rule that's kept him from going after the one woman he can't stop thinking about. Falling for Sophie could mean risking his oldest friendship. But walking away? That might be the biggest mistake of his life.

A sizzling, forbidden love, best friend's little sister romance packed with tension, heat, and undeniable chemistry!

***

Investigating Desire

A Slow-Burn Romantic Suspense with a Grumpy Detective and the Journalist Who Won't Back Down

Detective Nate Whitaker has sworn off love. After a messy divorce, he's buried himself in his work, content to keep his emotions locked away. But when a bold, relent-less journalist starts shadowing him for an exclusive story, their push-and-pull dynamic ignites a slow burn neither of them can ignore.

Tessa Donovan has worked hard to make a name for herself. She's determined to crack open a case that's rocked this small town, even if it means getting under the skin of a brooding detective who wants nothing to do with her. But when her investigation stirs up danger, Nate has no choice but to keep her close. What starts as a reluctant partnership turns into something far more dangerous—a fiery attraction neither of them is ready for.

With a growing threat looming and tension crackling between them, this small-town romantic suspense is about to heat up. Can Nate and Tessa untangle the case before it's too late, or will their undeniable chemistry turn into the biggest risk of all?

***

Falling for the Rescue

A Forced Proximity, Search and Rescue Romance Packed with Heat, Heart, and High Stakes

Ryan Anderson thrives in the chaos of Search and Rescue, risking everything to save those in danger. He's fierce-

ly independent, highly skilled, and never the one needing help—until a treacherous storm and a botched rescue
mission leave him stranded, injured, and facing the one
situation he can't control.

Enter Sam Monroe—a tough, no-nonsense ex-mili-
tary K9 handler who's spent years proving she doesn't
need anyone. Haunted by her past and more comfortable in survival mode than emotional entanglements, Sam
doesn't have time for distractions—especially not the kind
with broad shoulders, smoldering intensity, and a stubborn streak to match her own.

Forced to wait out the storm in a remote cabin in the
wilderness, their reluctant alliance turns into something
far more dangerous. Tensions ignite. Sparks fly. But neither of them is built for surrender—especially when old
wounds and hidden vulnerabilities threaten to unravel the
fragile trust between them.

**Will Sam and Ryan let down their walls and take a
risk on love? Or will fear and pride keep them from
the one person who finally sees them for who they
truly are?**

***

A Heart Worth Mending

Penelope Everett is chaos wrapped in sunshine and cinnamon. Milo Turner is a brooding small-town vet who prefers his solitude—and his scars—untouched.

But when an injured fox, a runaway goat, and a perfectly imperfect dance in a flour-dusted kitchen spark something real, Milo and Penelope are forced to face the truth: love isn't always neat. It's messy. It's brave. It's terrifying.

And sometimes... it's exactly what you need to heal.

Can a woman learning to choose herself risk everything on a man still learning how to stay?**A Heart Worth Mending is a small-town, age-gap romance packed with heart, heat, and a hero worth waiting for. Perfect for fans of grumpy-sunshine pairings, emotionally satisfying slow burns, and heroines who never stop believing in love—even when it hurts.**

***

***

Falling for the Billionaire Series

Hating Mr. Wentworth

They're supposed to be enemies—so why does arguing feel like foreplay?

Liz Bentley built her career on grit, caffeine, and a zero-tolerance policy for entitled men—especially not the newly appointed CEO with a famous last name and a face straight off a magazine cover. Brett Wentworth might be rich, polished, and maddeningly smug, but Liz knows his type: privilege, power, and betrayal wrapped in a designer suit.

Brett didn't ask to inherit the mess his father made of Bright Spark. But the moment Liz storms into his boardroom—all fire, wit, and defiance—he knows two things: she's the sharpest mind in the company... and the one woman he shouldn't want.

Their arguments are electric. Their chemistry, impossible to ignore. And one dangerously hot encounter changes everything. Now Brett has one shot to prove he's nothing like the men who came before—and everything Liz never saw coming.

Enemies on paper. Fireworks in person. A hot, hilarious romance that's one HR violation away from disaster—or the most delicious kind of downfall.

***

Tempting Mr. Dawson

A sizzling, laugh-out-loud billionaire romcom about mistaken identity, forbidden chemistry, and the hidden moment that might just lead to love.

Travel writer Piper Winslow is in paradise—but she's not here to relax. Her assignment? Review Coral Bay Resort and keep things strictly professional. But the guy in the Hawaiian shirt who offers her a "real" tour of the property? He's messing with her objectivity—and tempting her to break all her rules.

Logan Dawson didn't mean to lie. When Piper mistakes him for a charming staff member instead of the CEO of the luxury resort she's reviewing, he doesn't correct her. For once, someone sees him, not his title. And walking away from that? Not so easy.

What starts as playful banter turns into an afternoon of unforgettable heat in a hidden grotto. But when the truth comes out, so does the fallout. Now Logan has to prove that the man she fell for is the real him—and that what sparked between them wasn't just a vacation fling.

Tempting Mr. Dawson is a steamy billionaire romcom with sharp banter, tropical heat, mistaken identities, and a CEO who'll risk everything to win back the woman who saw through him.

***

Unraveling Mr. Ashford

Mia Wilder is a glitter bomb of chaos, creativity, and caffeine—and even she knows it's time for a vacation when her vision board catches fire. (Literally.)

So when a family friend pulls strings to score her a solo escape to a luxury island resort, Mia says yes—because nothing says self-care like seven days of sunshine, silence, and SPF 50.

Thanks to a booking snafu—and a storm that knocks out all communication—Mia finds herself stranded with Grant Ashford, a brooding tech billionaire who clearly didn't plan on sharing his R&R with an overcaffeinated sunbeam who narrates her inner monologue like it's a podcast.

He's grumpy, guarded, and allergic to distractions. She's sunshine in designer flip-flops. And neither of them is prepared for what happens next.

***

***

The Thorne Sisters Series

Ink & Iron

A grumpy, guarded veteran. A tattoo artist who turns pain into beauty. When trust feels like temptation, survival won't be enough.

Tanner Maddox didn't come to Briar Hill looking for second chances. He came to outrun the past, bury the guilt, and forget the wreckage he left behind. But one step into Needle & Ink—and one sharp-eyed artist who turns scars into stories—shatters every line he swore he wouldn't cross.

Lola Thorne knows better than to get tangled in someone else's broken pieces. She's got a tattoo shop to run, a past she won't talk about, and one rule she never breaks: don't fall for clients. Especially not a brooding ex-soldier with hands built for violence and a gaze that feels like a promise she can't afford to believe.

The tattoo was supposed to be just a cover. Instead, it uncovers the one thing neither of them thought they deserved: a future. He's all muscle, silence, and pain. She's all sharp edges, rough laughter, and a heart stitched together with ink and stubbornness. Together, they're something neither of them expected—and everything they didn't know how to want.

Walls will crumble. Rules will shatter. And when it's all stripped bare, the only thing left will be the truth—and the fight for a love worth every scar.

Ink & Iron is a steamy, emotional small-town romance about a grumpy veteran, a fierce tattoo artist, slow-burn tension, off-the-charts chemistry, and love so raw it leaves a mark deeper than skin.

***

Silk & Silence

She's built her world on control. He's forgotten what it means to want. But some sparks don't ask permission before they burn.

Vivian Thorne built her life on polish, power, and impeccable control. As the owner of the Velvet Room—a high-end burlesque club known for its vintage glamours—she knows how to captivate a crowd without ever letting anyone close. Love is a liability she can't afford—and perfection is the armor she never removes.

Dean Thatcher is a gruff, guarded divorce attorney who's seen every way love can break, bleed, and betray. He doesn't do risks. He doesn't do chaos. And he sure as hell doesn't fall for women who look like trouble wrapped in red lipstick and secrets.

Their connection should have been a brief spark—an impulse easy to ignore. But the more Dean uncovers the woman beneath the polish, the more he realizes she's the most dangerously real thing he's ever craved. And the more Vivian lets him in, the more terrified she is that he'll walk away when he sees the cracks no amount of armor can hide.Masks will slip. Hearts will break open. And when survival isn't enough anymore, they'll have to risk everything—for a love that strips them bare.

Silk & Silence is a steamy, emotional small-town romance about fierce vulnerability, slow-burn passion, and love without conditions. Perfect for fans of broken heroes, scarred heroines, emotional healing, and off-the-charts chemistry.

***

Pleasure & Prose

She's pure confidence and provocation. He's all restraint and repressed desire. But when opposites combust, even the rules don't stand a chance.

Simon Radcliffe is a buttoned-up British professor teaching at the local university, all nervous smiles and devastatingly proper manners. But when a wrong turn leads him through the doors of Pleasure & Co., he meets Veronica Thorne—a woman who exudes power, mystery, and the kind of sensual self-possession that makes him forget how to breathe.

Veronica doesn't do flustered. And she definitely doesn't go for repressed academics. But there's something about Simon—something curious and unguarded—that makes her pause. And when he asks her to tea—with the stiff sincerity of a man completely out of his depth—she says yes. Against every instinct, she says yes.

What begins as a slow, simmering pull becomes a wildfire neither of them is ready for. And when the past rears its nosy, unwelcome head, they'll have to decide what they're really fighting for.

Pleasure & Prose is a steamy, emotional small-town romance about opposites that ignite, slow burns that explode, and a cinnamon roll hero who learns the right woman doesn't just unravel you—she shows you who you've been all along.

***

Lessons & Leather

She's never been touched. He's never been trusted. But when a sunshine schoolteacher crashes into a broody mechanic—literally—the sparks don't stop flying.

Eliza Thorne has spent her whole life being good. Good daughter. Good sister. Good teacher. She keeps the peace, keeps things running, and keeps her deepest desires tucked safely out of sight. Wanting more has never felt like an option—until a fender bender introduces her to Clay Walker, the town's broodiest mechanic with a jaw that could cut glass and eyes that see far too much.

Clay doesn't do soft. Doesn't do complications. He keeps his head down, runs his garage, and avoids anything that might crack the armor he's spent years building. But Eliza Thorne—sunshine smile, cherry earrings, and quiet strength—doesn't just crack his walls. She dismantles them.

Their connection is electric. Impossible. Inevitable. But if they want more than just heat, they'll have to believe something neither of them has ever been told—that real love doesn't just hold space—it makes you feel like you belong in it.

Lessons & Leather is a steamy, small-town opposites-attract romance between a woman learning to

want and a man learning he's wanted. Featuring emotional firsts, protective tension, and the kind of slow burn that scorches when it finally ignites

***

***

The Men of Hawks Landing Series

Mountain Made

She came to the mountain to say goodbye. He was never part of the plan.

Anastasia Blake isn't running—at least, not in the way people think. The mountain cabin her grandmother left her was meant to be a quick project. Fix it. Sell it. Move on. But the moment she steps through the door, memories stir—of laughter, freedom, and the girl she used to be before the world told her who to become.

Travis Holt doesn't do drama, and he definitely doesn't do complications. But Anastasia? She's all sunlight and sharp edges, and she sees straight through the walls he's spent years perfecting. He's supposed to be there to help her leave—but the longer she stays, the harder it is to imagine letting her go. It was supposed to be easy. One moment. One goodbye. But some goodbyes aren't meant to be.

Mountain Made is a steamy, slow-burn romance about opposites who were never meant to attract, forced proximity that turns into something real, emotional healing, and a sexy mountain man who falls first and never looks back.

***

Mountain Found

Leaving the altar was the only decision she could make. Finding safety in the town's broodiest mechanic? That felt like fate.

Cal Mason wasn't looking for trouble. But trouble just took the room above his garage. Grace Sinclair didn't plan to become a runaway bride. But when forever with the wrong man became unbearable, she walked out mid-ceremony and kept driving until the mountains stopped her. Hawk's Landing was supposed to be a place to catch her breath—not to fall into the arms of a broody mechanic with hands that know how to rebuild broken things.

Cal Mason has no interest in complications. And Grace? She's nothing but complicated. Too polished. Too stubborn. Way too tempting. But when her past shows up at his door, Cal does what he's always done—protects what's his.

Her past wants her back. But Cal's already claimed her future.

Mountain Found is a steamy, emotional small-town romance about a runaway bride, a broody mechanic with a mile-wide protective streak, undeniable chemistry, and a love strong enough to stand against the past.

***

Mountain Promise

They were supposed to fake forever. Until he made her want the real thing.

Rowan McClaren has a plan: save her mother's legacy, keep the animal hospital running, and avoid needing anyone—especially a man. But when a legal loophole puts everything at risk, there's only one option left: marry someone. Fast.

Enter Miles Griffin—grumpy ex-soldier, resident plumber at Hawk's Landing Lodge, and the last person looking for a relationship. But when Rowan's quiet desperation meets Miles's steady

loyalty, they strike a deal: one marriage. One shared roof. No feelings.

It's supposed to be simple. But the longer Miles shares her space—the more he fixes what's broken and holds her like he means it—the harder it gets to remember what's fake. Because falling for Miles Griffin wasn't part of the deal. But it might be the only thing that makes sense now.

Mountain Promise is a steamy, slow-burn small-town romance about a grumpy ex-soldier, a fiercely independent heroine, one fake "I do," and the real love they never saw coming.

***

Mountain Kept

She's his best friend's little sister—vibrant, fearless,and completely off-limits. He's the town flirt who's never let anyone close...until her.

Lucy Griffin is tired of being the afterthought. Bold and full of life, she wants more than surface-level affection—she wants something real. And the only person who's ever made her feel truly seen? The one man she's never supposed to want.

Eli Granger hides behind charm and easy grins. He doesn't do complicated. Doesn't do commitment. And definitely doesn't mess around with Miles Griffin's little sister. But when Lucy shows up in Hawk's Landing and turns his carefully curated life upside down, every rule starts to crack.

Then a storm leaves them stranded together in the woods—and one night changes everything.

She wants to be chosen. He's terrified to want anything real. And falling for her could cost him the only family he's ever known.

A steamy, small-town best friend's sister romance with forbidden tension, slow-burn heat, and a flirty hero who finally meets his match.

***

To stay up to date on all of my releases, subscribe to my mailing list here!

www.ingramcontent.com/pod-product-compliance
Lightning Source LLC
Chambersburg PA
CBHW051254170626
46809CB00004B/1646